The Clumsies
make a mess

First published in paperback in
Great Britain by
HarperCollins Children's Books 2010

HarperCollins Children's Books is a
division of HarperCollins*Publishers* Ltd
77-85 Fulham Palace Road,
Hammersmith, London W6 8JB

The HarperCollins website address is:
www.harpercollins.co.uk

1

Printed and bound in England by Clays Ltd,
St Ives plc

Copyright © Sorrel Anderson 2010
Illustrations © Nicola Slater 2010
Designed by Tracey Hurst

ISBN: 978-0-00-733090-4

CONFIDENTIAL

By ~~Sorrel Anderson~~ Klumsiez

The Clumsies

make a mess

Illustrated by Nicola Slater

HarperCollins Children's Books

For Purvis and Mickey Thompson

Contents

t was a Tuesday morning and everything was just as it usually was. As usual, Howard Armitage arrived at his office at a quarter to nine. As usual, he bought

a cup of coffee and two sausages
from the office canteen.
Then, as usual, he set off down
the long corridor . . . . .

. . . to his room.

Suddenly there was a

booming

voice behind him.

'ARMITAGE!' it said.

It was Mr Bullerton, Howard's boss.

'Hello, Mr Bullerton,' said Howard.

'Hmph,' said Mr Bullerton, crossly. 'I've just been in your room, and it's a *mess.* As usual.'

3

'Oh, I—' began Howard.

'Why is it?' said Mr Bullerton.

'Well, err—'

'I won't have it,' said Mr Bullerton.

'No, I—'

'Tidy it!' said Mr Bullerton.

He gave Howard's sausage-box a nasty look and his nostrils, which were large, gave a twitch.

'What's in the box?'

'Sausages,' said Howard.

'**Sausages?**' spluttered Mr Bullerton. 'I hope you're not intending to eat sausages in your office.'

'Err, I—'

'No eating at desks!' said Mr Bullerton. 'It's unhygienic!'

'Yes, Mr Bullerton,' said Howard.

'And untidy!'

'Yes, Mr Bullerton,' said Howard.

'Desks are for **working** on, **not eating off.** Any eating to be done will be done in the canteen and in the canteen *only*.

'Especially sausages,'

said Mr Bullerton. 'Well, go on then.'

Howard went back to the canteen, waited until Mr Bullerton had gone, and then took his breakfast to his room, just as he always did. He was about to take a large bite of sausage when there was a rustling noise.

'That's unusual,' said Howard, and the noise stopped. Then it started again, loudly.

There was something under the desk, *and it was moving.*

Howard sprang upwards and backwards and peered underneath. There was a bag, and it was twitching. He **prodded** it and something small and round **SHOT** out.

'Squeeep!'

it said.

'Tut,' said Howard. 'A mouse.'

The mouse hurtled off into the corner and Howard sat back down. He was about to take a large bite

of sausage when there was another rustling noise.

'Now look,' said Howard. 'I've had just about enough of this.' He kicked

the bag and another

mouse **popped** out, smaller and **rounder** than the first. It started to trundle away, glancing nervously at Howard over its shoulder.

'You may well glance at me nervously,' said Howard, picking up an empty water glass and placing it over the mouse.

'You'll stay in there so I can eat my breakfast in peace. I shall deal with you afterwards.'

Howard sat back down and had just taken a **large** mouthful of coffee when something **bashed** his ankle.

It was the first mouse, back again. 'Let him out!' squealed the mouse, *pummelling*.

Howard choked 🍃

on his coffee, and the mouse stopped pummelling.

'*Please*, I mean. *Please* let him out, Howard Armitage,' said the mouse.

Howard made a **gargling** noise, and the mouse giggled.

'Here, you've got coffee all down your chin,' he said, passing Howard a small tissue.

'So would you, if you'd been sprung at all over the place and *pummelled*,' said Howard, mopping.

'Sorry,' said the mouse. 'It was the biscuits.'

'*What* was the biscuits?' said Howard.

'They were in that bag,' said the mouse, 'and we, err, *borrowed* some, and fell asleep. If I get you some more, will you let my brother go?'

'I don't want *biscuits*,' said Howard. 'I want **sausages**.'

'I'll get you some sausages then,' offered the mouse.

'I've already *got* sausages,' said Howard. 'All I need now is a bit of calm in which to eat them. Is that too much to ask?'

'Not at all,' said the mouse.

'Well, quite,' said Howard.

Sighing, Howard lifted the water glass and the smaller, rounder mouse scuttled out, looking a bit hot and *very* relieved.

'Thank you,' said the first mouse. 'We'll be off then,' and he started bundling his brother away.

'One second,' said Howard. 'How do you know my name's Howard Armitage?'

'There's a sign on your door that says:

"Howard Armitage",
said the mouse, 'so I assumed.'

'Did you now?' said Howard,
narrowing his eyes.

'Isn't it then?' asked the mouse,
sounding confused.

'As a matter of fact it is,' said
Howard. 'I think you'd better tell
me who you are.'

'He's Mickey Thompson,' said
the mouse, **poking** his
brother's tummy.

'*I* can tell him,' said Mickey
Thompson, **wriggling**,

and poking his brother back.

'I'm Mickey Thompson,' announced Mickey Thompson, to Howard.

'Pleased to meet you, Mickey Thompson,' said Howard.

'And I'm Purvis,' said the first mouse, **thumping** himself on the chest.

'Purvis what?' said Howard.

'Purvis what?' said Purvis.

'Or what Purvis?' said Howard.

'*That* Purvis,' said Mickey Thompson. 'There's only one, and he's him.' Mickey Thompson

prodded Purvis in the ribs, and there was a small scuffle.

Howard's head was beginning to throb. **'That's enough, you two,'** said Howard. **'When you're in my office you'll behave, or I shall put you under that glass again.'**

Purvis and Mickey Thompson behaved.

'That's better,' said Howard. He
went over to a side table and

cla t t ere d
about,

putting the
kettle on

. . . and finding

two extra mugs.

'Tea?'

'Yes please,' said Purvis.

'Have you got any juice?' asked Mickey Thompson.

'No,' said Howard. 'It's tea or cold coffee.'

'Tea please,' said Mickey Thompson, pulling a face. 'Have you got any more biscuits?'

'Don't push your luck,' said Howard.

While Howard made the tea the mice climbed up on to his desk and had a look around.

'It's a bit messy up here,' called Purvis, ruffling through piles of paper. 'Would you like me to help you tidy it up?'

'Absolutely not,' said Howard.
'Leave everything exactly as it is.'
There was a loud
crash
as Mickey Thompson

slid off a stack of books,

knocked over a box of pens....

and landed
in a pot
plant.

Howard rushed over.

'Oops!' said Mickey
Thompson, happily.

'Sorry!' said Purvis, hauling him
out.

'Will you be careful,' said
Howard. 'I'm fond of that plant.'

'Yes, it's *lovely*,' said Purvis,
trying to jam a flower back on its
stalk.

'Could I have a piece of that
sausage, do you think?' asked
Mickey Thompson, eyeing it.

'Oh, go on then,' sighed
Howard. 'Help yourself.'

So Mickey Thompson tucked
into Howard's breakfast while
Purvis swept pieces of plant on to
the floor, and Howard fetched the
mugs of tea.

'Right,' said Howard. 'You'd better tell me why you're here.'

'We live here,' explained Purvis.

Howard closed his eyes and made a ***groaning*** noise.

'Why are you groaning?' asked Mickey Thompson, cheerfully.

'Where's *"here"*?' said Howard.

'Err, here in this building,' said Purvis.

'*Where* in this building?' pressed Howard.

'Under your desk,' said Mickey Thompson.

'Because,' Purvis continued quickly, 'we thought it seemed like a very nice place.' 'Biscuits!'

said Mickey Thompson, helpfully.

'And you seem like a very nice man,' said Purvis, hopefully.

'H'rumph,' said Howard Armitage.

'And there isn't really anywhere else we can go,' said Purvis, studying his tea.

Howard sighed. 'Oh, yes, all right then,' he said. 'You can stay.'

'*Hurray!*' said Mickey Thompson. 'Can I have some more sausage?'

'If you must,' said Howard, getting up. 'Right. I've got to go to a meeting. Don't touch anything on that desk while I'm away.'

'How about under it?' asked Purvis.

'Fine,' said Howard.

So Howard went off to his meeting and the two mice

28

started **rummaging** underneath the desk.

By the time Howard got back there was a large pile of **clutter** in the middle of the room. Propped against it was a LONG

cardboard tube, which the mice
were busy using in a game.

'Look, Howard!' called Mickey
Thompson, *sliding down the tube*

and landing at Howard's feet.

'I can see!' said Howard.

'Are there any more cardboard
tubes?' asked Purvis, **puffing**
slightly.

'I expect so,' said Howard. 'Why?'

'If we could make the course **bigger**,' we could win more points,' said Purvis.

'I'll see what I can find,' said Howard. 'How do you win the points, anyway?'

Purvis took a deep breath. 'You have to go round, over and through; through, round and over; over, round and through;

over, through and round;
round, through and over;
through, over and round,

in the right order; then you do it all again in a different right order and after that it gets difficult to explain.'

Howard shuddered.

'Well, we've started now,' said Purvis, 'so we might as well get to the end!'

'If you say so,' said Howard.

He left them to it and went to fetch the cardboard tubes from the storeroom, which was d
o
w
n
a corridor, **along** a corridor, and **up** a flight of stairs. But when he arrived, the door wouldn't open.

'That's funny,' muttered Howard, rattling the handle. He put his shoulder against the door and **shoved**.

It **crashed** open and
Howard *tipped in, tripped over,*

and landed
flat on the floor.
There was a **TOOTING** noise.

'Was that me?' wondered
Howard. The tooting happened
again, louder and nearer.

'That wasn't me,' said
Howard. He got up, carefully.

'TRUMPET!!!'
went the noise, *very loud*
and extremely near.

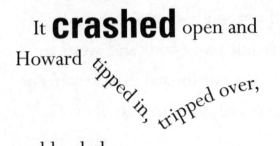

34

Howard ju^{m}ped and **bumped** his head. Then something tapped him on the bottom. It was an elephant. 'Concussion? This. Is it?' said Howard, staggering. He shut his eyes, counted to five and opened them again, but the elephant was still there. It was a remarkably small one, about the size of a Labrador puppy. It looked eager, and slightly apologetic.

'Err, hello,' said Howard. The elephant gazed at him, and said nothing.

'Hmm,' said Howard. He scooped up some cardboard tubes and went towards the door.

'Well, goodbye then.'

'TOOT! TRUMPET! TOOOOT!'

went
the
elephant,
and
ran
after
him.

'Oh dear,' sighed Howard. 'Yes. All right.'

The stairs to the storeroom were

narrow and s t e e p.

They stood at the top and looked down. 'There's nothing to worry about,' said Howard. 'I'll go in front and you follow me.'

Howard

     started

        down

          the stairs and the elephant stayed where she was.

'Come on now,' said Howard, encouragingly.

The elephant didn't move.

'Come along,' said Howard, coaxingly.

The elephant backed away.

'Come!' ordered Howard, exasperatedly. The elephant gave a panicked

TRUMPET,

did a little run backwards and forwards and launched herself off the top stair on to Howard's chest.

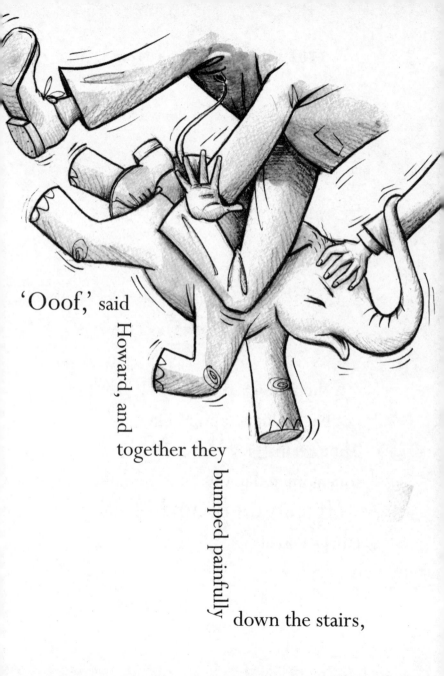

'Ooof,' said Howard, and together they bumped painfully down the stairs, and bumped,

even more painfully,

on to the floor

at the bottom.

When Howard and the elephant

got back, Purvis and Mickey

Thompson bounced over,

squeaking excitedly:

'It's an elephant! It's an elephant!'

'Less of it,' said Howard.

'Why are you all hot in the face,
Howard?' asked Mickey Thompson.

'Mickey Thompson,' said
Howard, breathing heavily. 'So far
today I've **bashed** my shoulder,
hit my head, had my bottom
prodded and my stomach
squashed. I've been **bumped**
downstairs and **bumped**, hard,
on to the floor. There's a pair
of talking mice living under
my desk and now there's an
elephant too. *That's* why I'm
hot in the face. Now, somebody

put the kettle on

while I think

what to do.'

'She's only a baby,' said Purvis.
'We must look after her.'
'Very probably,' said Howard,

'but I don't know what she'll eat.'

'Buns,' said Mickey Thompson, quickly.

'No, that's what *you* eat,' said Purvis.

'Elephants like buns. I read it,' said Mickey Thompson.

'In a storybook,' said Purvis.

Mickey Thompson blew a *raspberry* at Purvis and there was a small scuffle.

'Stop,' said Howard. 'You're jangling my bruises.'

'I think we should look it up,' said Purvis. So they looked it up.

'Elephants eat **grass**, **small branches** and **bark** from trees,' read out Purvis.

'Yuk!' said Mickey Thompson.

'Fabulous,' said Howard.

'They especially like leaves from the top branches,' he continued.

'Take a look around,' said Howard. 'How many branches do you see in here, top or otherwise?'

'Hang on,' said Purvis. 'It also

says they like *fruit*, *vegetables* *and seeds*.' The elephant **TRUMPETED** in agreement.

'That's more like it,' said Howard. 'I'll go to the canteen.'

So he went, and came back carrying:

Seven apples

Three boxes of vegetable stir fry

and one of cauliflower cheese

A small packet of
something called
'*Nibbly
McCrunchie's
Snacking Seeds*'

Two new sausages

and a bag of buns.
They spread it
all out on the
floor like a
picnic and
everyone tucked in.

'What shall we call this elephant
then?' said Howard.

'What about *Howard?*' said
Mickey Thompson, and he and
Purvis fell about

giggling.

'Certainly not,' said Howard.

'What about Ortrud?' said
Purvis.

'Why Ortrud?' said Howard.

'No particular reason, I just happen to like the name,' said Purvis.

'Me too,' said Howard. 'I had an Auntie Ortrud who used to make delicious *chocolate cake*.'

'Did she make any other kinds of cake?' asked Mickey Thompson, interestedly.

'Yes, Mickey Thompson, she did,' said Howard.

'Did she make *apple cake*?' asked Mickey Thompson.

'Yes,' said Howard.

'What about *apple pie?*'

'Yes, and *apple pie,*' said Howard. 'She was a keen baker. Whatever is the matter Purvis?'

'What about *flapjacks?*' said Mickey Thompson.

'*Shush*, Mickey Thompson,' said Purvis, 'there's someone coming!'

The mice and Ortrud dived under the desk . . . .

just as the door opened and Mr
Bullerton came in.

'Armitage, I...' began Mr
Bullerton. Then he stopped and
stared at Howard, who was still
sitting on the floor surrounded by
cardboard tubes and picnic. Mr
Bullerton grew redder and redder
and eventually started shouting:

'I said NO EATING. And what
are all these CARDBOARD
TUBES? Have you gone
COMPLETELY MAD?'

'No, I, err, well...' said
Howard.

'*WELL?*'
thundered
Mr Bullerton.

'I'm right in the middle of tidying up,' said Howard. 'It'll be better soon.'

'It'd better be,' said Mr Bullerton, 'and by the end of the day, or you're **fired**. And I need you to go to the next meeting. *Now*.'

'But I can't tidy up if I'm in the meeting,' said Howard, reasonably.

'That's your problem,' said Mr Bullerton.

'Get going.'

'Poor Howard!' said Purvis, once they'd gone. 'We must help.'

'But there's so much mess,' said Mickey Thompson, 'and hardly any time.'

'Let's shove it all in here,' said Purvis, **yanking** open the cupboard door. So the mice and Ortrud bustled back and forth cramming all the mess from Howard's room into Howard's cupboard and filing cabinet.

'The room seems bigger now,' said Mickey Thompson, once they'd finished.

'And dustier,' sneezed
Purvis.

So they found
some
dusters

and a large can of furniture polish,
and squirted it all over the desk,
and the walls, and the window,
and the floor. After a lot of
rubbing everything looked
better, and shinier.

'Whee!' said Mickey
Thompson, twirling around.

'*I'm skating!*'

'**TOOOOT!**' went Ortrud, joining in.

'Quick!' said Purvis. 'They're coming!'

They all dived under the desk just as Howard and Mr Bullerton appeared in the doorway.

'Oh!' said Howard, sounding surprised.

'Oh!' said Mr Bullerton, sounding disappointed. 'Hmph, well, this is better. You're not fired then, I suppose. For now.'

Mr Bullerton **stomped** off, and Howard stepped into the room, skidded, and landed on his bottom, **very hard**.

'Whoosh!' said Mickey Thompson, appreciatively, as Howard slid across the shiny floor, very fast.

'Whoops!' said Purvis, worriedly, as Howard **crashed**, and the cupboard door sprang open, and a huge muddle of

boxes and biscuits and paper and pens and cardboard tubes and bits of bun cascaded out on top of him.

'*Yoooou............. CLUMSIES!!!*' bellowed Howard, muffledly, from underneath the **heap**.

'Oh well!' said Mickey Thompson. 'It's nice having the room back to normal again.'

'Yes!' said Purvis. 'I think I'll put the kettle on.'

t was very cold in the office.

'*Brrr,*' said Purvis. 'It's *freezing.*'

'Yes, *brrr,*' said Mickey Thompson, looking at Howard.

'*Brrr. Brrr. BRRR.*'

Howard ignored them and carried on typing.

'*BRRRRRRRR*,' said Mickey Thompson.

'**TRUMPET**,' said Ortrud, joining in.

'Will. You. *SHOOSH*,' said Howard. 'I'm trying to finish this report. It's late.'

'But it's so cold, Howard,' said Purvis. '*Brrr. Brrr.*'

'*Brrr*,' said Mickey Thompson.

'*Brrr*,' said Purvis.

'**TOOT**,' said Ortrud.

'Tut,' said Howard, and stopped typing. 'I know you're cold,' he said.

'I know I know I know. *I'm* cold too. I'm *so* cold I can hardly *move*. I'm *so* cold I can hardly *type*. And you lot are making *so* much racket I can *hardly think*.'

He got up and fetched his coat.

'Good idea,' said Purvis. 'We'll wrap Ortrud in it.'

'I was going to wrap *me* in it,' muttered Howard, as he helped the mice drape it over Ortrud.

'Can I wear *this*?'
asked Purvis,
pulling a woolly
scarf out of one
of the pockets.

'I expect so,' said Howard.

'And can I wear *this*?'
asked Mickey
Thompson,
pulling a woolly
hat out of the
other pocket.

'Would you like the shirt off my back too?' said Howard, through **gritted teeth**.

'Won't that make you even *colder*?' asked Purvis, sounding concerned.

'Wear these, Howard!' said Mickey Thompson, holding up a pair of mittens.

Sighing, Howard took them,
and put them on.

'Mind you, it's going to be
tricky typing in mittens,' said
Mickey Thompson to Purvis, and
they both
giggled.

'Let's have some *hush* while
I get on with this,' said Howard,
and he started to type again,
s l o w l y .

'Why is it *so cold*, anyway,
Howard?' asked Purvis.

The radiator made a
banging,

clanking noise and everyone **jumped.** That's why,' said Howard. 'The boiler isn't working properly.'

Suddenly there was a different kind of **banging noise** and the Clumsies dived *under the desk* just as Mr Bullerton BURST into the room.

He was wearing a hat,

and a
coat,
and a
scarf,

and some gloves.

'Where is it?' he *barked*.

'I'm doing it now, Mr Bullerton,' said Howard.

'It's supposed to be done already,' said Mr Bullerton.

'I know,' said Howard, 'but—'

'Well, why isn't it?

'It's so cold,' said Howard, his teeth

chattering.

'I'm having trouble

t y p i n g.'

70

Mr Bullerton stared at Howard and then at Howard's hands.

'Mittens?' he squawked. '*Mittens*? You can't type in mittens.'

'Well, it isn't easy, but—'

'Take them off,' said Mr Bullerton.

'But if—'

'Off!' said Mr Bullerton. 'OFF!'

'But if I take them off, my fingers will freeze,' said Howard.

Mr Bullerton stuck his face very close to Howard's.

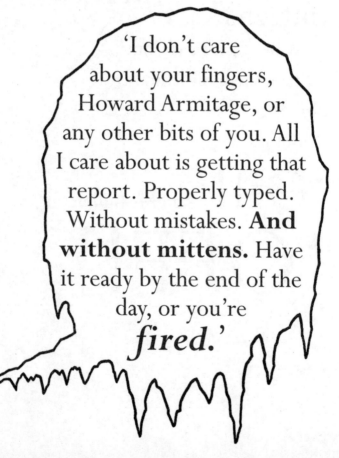

'I don't care about your fingers, Howard Armitage, or any other bits of you. All I care about is getting that report. Properly typed. Without mistakes. **And without mittens.** Have it ready by the end of the day, or you're *fired.*'

Howard began typing frantically, and Mr Bullerton stalked out of the room.

Purvis and Mickey Thompson looked at each other.

'Poor Howard!' said Mickey Thompson.

'We must find that boiler, and fix it,' said Purvis. 'Let's start at the radiator and work backwards.'

Next to the radiator was a small hole in the wall, so they climbed into it. Inside the wall was a long silvery pipe with an official-looking sign on it.

'What does it say?' asked Mickey Thompson.

Purvis stood on Mickey Thompson's back to get a better look.

"SECTOR B (LOWER) ACCESS ONLY LAST INSP 9.89 REF JPJ,"

read out Purvis.

'Gerromff!' said Mickey Thompson, muffledly.

'Eh?' said
Purvis,
climbing off.

'I said, "would you mind ever so slightly getting off me now please thank you",' said Mickey Thompson. 'What do you think it means?'

'It doesn't seem to make any sense at all,' said Purvis.

'Maybe we should go back then,' said Mickey Thompson. 'It must be nearly tea time.'

'You've only just had your lunch,' said Purvis. 'Come on.' So they climbed into the pipe and slid down and around and around and down . . .

. . . for what seemed a very long time.

'Whee!' said Mickey Thompson, who was enjoying himself.

'Whoa!' said Purvis,

who was beginning to feel anxious
about whether they'd ever reach
the end, and what they'd find there
if they did.

But eventually they arrived in the basement. They'd never been this far **d**
o
w
n in the building before. It was *gloomy* and **cold** and *echoey* and smelt of damp and feet. Purvis shivered.
Through thick clouds of yellowy grey steam they saw an

e n o r m o u s,

dome-shaped thing. It was made of rusty metal and was covered in dust and soot.

There were a lot of pipes going into it and a lot of other pipes coming out of it and it was topped off with a coMplicAted arrangement of bellows, springs and dials.

'Wow,' breathed Purvis. 'The boiler.' He walked all the way around and fetched up in front of the largest of the dials.

'Hello!' said the boiler. Purvis jumped backwards and Mickey

Thompson shot underneath a
nearby cupboard. 'Um… may I
help you?' asked the boiler,
politely.

'Well,' said Purvis. 'I'm Purvis.
And he's Mickey Thompson.' He
nodded in that direction and
Mickey Thompson reappeared, and
waved.

'I'm Bernie,' said the boiler.

'We've come to fix you,'
announced Mickey Thompson.

'Oh yes?' said Bernie, nervously.

'Yes,' confirmed Purvis. 'The
building's *freezing* cold and

Howard says it's because you're not working properly, which means *he* can't work properly, which means there'll be **trouble** from Mr Bullerton.'

'Oh dear,' said Bernie, dissolving into a fit of

coughing,

which made his pressure gauges rise alarmingly and steam

shoot out.

Everything shook and there was the sound of pipes **hammering** in the distance.

82

Purvis handed up a
tissue.

'I'm all bunged up,'
said Bernie. He *sneezed*
five times and sniffed
loudly.

'That'll be what's causing it,'
said Purvis, nodding. 'Don't worry
– we shall *un-bung* you.'

'Oo,' said Bernie, 'Righty-o.
Err… how?'

'Um…' said Purvis.

'Yes?' said Bernie.

'Well…' said Purvis.

'With our un-bunging

equipment,' said Mickey Thompson.

'Exactly,' said Purvis. 'We'll go and fetch it now.' They started to go towards the door.

'Wait!' said Bernie. They stopped.

'While you're at it, I don't suppose you could bring me a little something, could you?'

'Of course,' said Purvis. 'What would you like?'

'Hot blackcurrant juice, please,' said Bernie.

'OK,' said Purvis. 'Back soon.' They set off again.

'Wait!' said Bernie. They
stopped again.

'And a chicken sandwich.'

'No problem,' said Purvis.
'Won't be long.' They set off again.

'Oh, err…' said Bernie.
They stopped again. 'Or maybe a
chocolate-spread sandwich…'

'How about chicken *and*
chocolate-spread?' suggested
Mickey Thompson.

'Fine,' agreed Bernie. 'And
some—'

'*Bye!*' said Purvis, bustling Mickey
Thompson out of the basement.

'Crisps,' said Bernie, as they hurried away. 'Is there any cake?' he called after them, hopefully.

When they got back to the office Howard had gone to a meeting and Ortrud was waiting for them.

'Right,' said Purvis. 'Ortrud and I will go and find things while you make the sandwiches.'

There was a bit of a squabble about whether Bernie had wanted the chicken and chocolate-spread to be separate or together but Mickey Thompson said he'd do some of each to be on the safe side.

'It's a pity about the cake,' said Purvis. 'I think we finished it all yesterday.'

'There's a piece of sponge cake in Howard's desk drawer, actually,' **blurted** out Mickey Thompson.

Purvis and Ortrud looked at Mickey Thompson and Mickey Thompson looked a bit sheepish.

'Err, I just happened to notice it,' he explained, trying to sound casual.

Everyone agreed that Howard would want Bernie to have his cake, so Mickey Thompson went off to fetch it.

'And don't eat any of it, Mickey Thompson,' called Purvis.

'I won't!'
protested
Mickey Thompson,
huffily.

In half an hour they met back and examined what they'd gathered, which was a lot. Purvis had:

A bucket

A broom

A bottle of
extra-strength,
lemon-scented
washing-up liquid

Washing
Up
Liquid

A tin of *Mr Buff-it-up* furniture
polish (marked *Best before Oct 1987*)

and a
large
pair of pants.

'Whose are those?' asked Mickey Thompson.

'Mr Bullerton's,' said Purvis. 'He goes to the gym at lunchtime, and changes.'

'But what are they for?' asked Mickey Thompson.

'*Buffing*,' said Purvis. 'They're nice and soft. Ortrud found them in his office.'

Ortrud **TRUMPETED**, proudly.

Mickey Thompson had made Bernie a get-well card with a picture of a cup of tea on it, and a picnic of:

Three kinds of sandwich
(chicken, chocolate-spread,
chicken *and* chocolate-spread)

Two flavours of crisps (*Salt 'n'
Vinegar* and *Cheese 'n' Onion*)

A large tartan flask of hot blackcurrant juice

and a carrot.

He had also found Howard's slice of sponge cake, which had pink icing with hundreds and thousands on top and was, as he pointed out, still in its cellophane wrapper.

They bundled everything on to Ortrud and led her over to the hole in the wall.

They looked at the hole and then at Ortrud.

'I don't think she'll fit,' said Mickey Thompson.

Ortrud looked a bit crestfallen.

'Never mind,' said Purvis. 'We'll just have to go the office way. They've all gone to the meeting so it should be OK.'

So they climbed on to Ortrud and set off.

Purvis was right — there was no
one around.

Swaying *slightly*, the Clumsies
started down the empty corridor,
picking up speed as they rounded
the corner.

Ortrud's load was beginning to tilt dangerously just as they reached the lift, but luckily the doors opened with a ping and they fell inside.

'Where to?' said the lift.

'Basement please,' said Purvis, and

suddenly the floor seemed to fall

from beneath them as they

whooshed

downwards

very

fast.

'*YEEEEEEEEEP!*'

said the mice. The lift came to a **sudden stop**, hovered for a moment or two and then *whooshed* back up again.

'*SQUEEEEEEEEEEEEP!*'

said the mice and **'TRUMPET!'** said Ortrud.

'Oops, sorry, silly me,' tittered the lift, and *whooshed* them down again so quickly that no one had time to say anything at all

before the doors *pinged* open
and they   tumbled

                            out

                            in

                            a

                          heap

on to the basement floor.

'Byeee!' called the lift, **whooshing** off again.

Bernie was pleased to see them and *even more* pleased with his picnic, so Mickey Thompson fed pieces of food into him while Purvis carefully poured the washing-up liquid over Bernie's top and sides and into all his pipes. Then Ortrud *squirted*

water at him with her trunk, and they started **scrubbing.**

It was a difficult job: Bernie was
very dirty, very ticklish and got the
hiccups.

'Eek! Hic!
Ooo! Hic!
You're
tick…hic!…ling!

Hic! Nooo!
Eee! Hic!
Hic! Ooo!'

he hooted. There was a loud

bang, and Bernie had to
have three cups of hot blackcurrant
poured in before it was safe to
carry on. But eventually he was
covered in a huge cloud of lemony
bubbles. So were the Clumsies and
most of the basement.

'How are you feeling now,
Bernie?' asked Purvis.

'Still a bit blocked in my main
out-pipe, I'm afraid,' said Bernie,
stuffily.

'Don't worry,' said Purvis.

'Ortrud can blow up it. That
should shift things.'

Meanwhile, the rest of the building was starting to feel warm, and damp. Howard came back from his meeting and began typing again. As the building got hotter and wetter, Howard typed *faster* and *faster.* He had just finished the report when the door opened and Mr Bullerton **squelched** in.

'It's done!' said Howard.

'Hmph,' said Mr Bullerton, sounding disappointed. 'Yes, well, I don't need that any more – I forgot to tell you. But what's all this?'

He flapped
his hands about.

'All what,
Mr Bullerton?' said Howard,
tiredly, as a large droplet of water
fell from the ceiling and splashed off Mr Bullerton's head.

105

'THIS!' snapped Mr Bullerton. 'Wetness. And *mess*. *Look!*'

Howard looked. There were puddles of water on the carpet, and trickles of water down the walls, and a lot of bubbles floating about.

'Oh dear,' said Howard.
Then the radiator started

banging

and

clanking

again, very

loudly.

'THERE'S SOMETHING
WRONG WITH YOUR
RADIATOR,' shouted Mr
Bullerton.

'OH DEAR,' shouted Howard.

'DON'T KEEP
SAYING "OH DEAR",'

shouted Mr Bullerton. 'DO SOMETHING.'

'LIKE WHAT?' shouted Howard.

'HIT IT!' shouted Mr Bullerton.

'I'm not sure that's—'

'NOW!' shouted Mr Bullerton, to Howard.

'*NOW!*' shouted Purvis, to Ortrud.

Ortrud **blew**, Howard **hit**, and… a great jet of lemony, bubbly, chickeny, chocolatey blackcurrantiness **burst** out

of the radiator, all over Howard
and Mr Bullerton.

'Ooh, that feels much better,'
said Bernie, happily.

When the Clumsies got back
to Howard's room, Howard
was sitting in his chair looking
purple, and *sticky,* and
CrOSS.

'Howard!' said Purvis.

'Purvis!' said Howard.

'We've been mending the boiler!' said Mickey Thompson, brightly.

'I thought you probably had,' said Howard.

'So, did you finish the report?' asked Purvis, putting the kettle on.

'Yes,' said Howard.'

'And did Mr Bullerton like it?'

'No,' said Howard. 'He's gone home. For a bath.'

'We've got his pants,' said Mickey Thompson.

Howard closed his eyes, and made a **groaning** noise.

'Hurry up with that tea. And pass me the cake I've been saving. I need it.'

The Clumsies looked at each other.

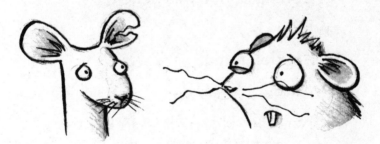

'Err,' said Purvis.

'What now?' said Howard.

'We fed it to Bernie, the boiler,' said Mickey Thompson.

'We knew you'd want him to have it,' said Purvis.

'And he wasn't well,' said Mickey Thompson.

'And he said it was delicious,' said Purvis.

'I'm delighted,' *sighed* Howard, sneezing, as a large, yellow bubble landed on his nose and went POP.

The Waggiest Tail

part 1

ne day, Howard Armitage seemed even more distracted than usual. He kept *sighing,* and

gazing

out of the window.

115

Purvis
made
him
a
cup
of
tea,

but he let it go cold. Mickey
Thompson brought him a sausage,

but he let that go cold too.

Then they tried **clattering**
up and down on his computer

keyboard —which usually attracted attention — but he just carried on *sighing* and gazing.

'Howard,' said Purvis, eventually. 'Is there anything wrong?'

'Yes,' said Howard. 'I'm worried about Allen, my dog.'

'Oo! I didn't know you had a dog,' said Purvis.

'I think he might be a bit depressed,' said Howard. 'He keeps *sighing* and gazing out of the window.'

The Clumsies exchanged glances.

'Maybe we could *cheer* him up?' suggested Purvis. 'Why don't you bring him in with you tomorrow?'

'Err, pleasant dog, is he?' asked Mickey Thompson, trying to sound casual.

'He's a very pleasant dog,' confirmed Howard.

'That's settled then,' said Purvis. 'We'll *play* with him, and give him tea.'

So the next day, Howard brought
Allen into the office and left him
with the Clumsies while he went
off to a meeting. Over a pot of tea
the mice asked Allen whether
there was anything worrying him,
and Allen sighed.

'I've got myself into
a tight spot,' he
explained.

'That happens to us quite often too,' said Mickey Thompson, cheerfully.

'What kind of a tight spot?' asked Purvis.

'I've gone and agreed to take part in a competition,' said Allen, 'and I'm *dreading* it.'

'What kind of a competition?' asked Purvis.

Allen handed over a crumpled piece of paper. Printed on it were the words:

DOG WITH THE WAGGIEST TAIL COMPETITION!!!

SATURDAY 1st MAY

FIRST PRIZE:
A YEAR'S SUPPLY OF BISCUITS!!!

SECOND PRIZE:
A WEEK'S SUPPLY OF BISCUITS!!

THIRD PRIZE:
A PACKET OF BISCUITS!

'*Wow!*' breathed Mickey Thompson. 'Don't you like biscuits?'

'Yes,' said Allen, 'but I don't enjoy competing. Competitions make me very anxious, and when I'm anxious my tail won't wag.'

'But surely Howard won't make you, if you don't want to?' said Purvis.

'No,' said Allen, 'but I don't want to disappoint him. He's *very excited* about it.'

'Oh dear,' said Purvis.

'Yes,' said Allen, glumly.

Everyone sipped their tea, and thought.

'I know!' said Mickey Thompson. 'We'll hide the advert, and then Howard will forget all about it.'

'I don't think he will,' said Allen. 'He's written it up on the calendar in the kitchen.'

Everyone sipped their tea some more, and thought some more.

'I know!' said Purvis. 'On the day of the competition, you can pretend you feel *queasy*. Then Howard will let you stay in bed.'

'I'm not sure that would work either,' said Allen. 'He might take me to the vet, and that would be just as bad.'

'And if he thinks you're feeling *queasy* he might not give you any dinner,' said Mickey

Thompson, 'and that would be *even worse*.'

Everyone agreed that would be *even worse*. They all sipped harder, and thought harder.

'I know!' said Purvis, *leaping up*.

'We'll disguise Ortrud as you, and she can take part in the competition in your place.'

Everyone studied Ortrud.

'She's about the same size,' mused Allen.

'And roughly the same shape,' said Purvis.

'Not at the front she isn't,' said
Mickey Thompson,
pulling Ortrud's
trunk.

'We can do something about
that,' called Purvis, rummaging in
the **clutter** under Howard's desk.
Ortrud
TRUMPETED, and
backed away.

'Don't worry, Ortrud,' said
Purvis. 'We won't get rid of it
completely – we'll just hide it.
Look.'

He dragged out a large cardboard box.

Everyone looked at the box, and then at Purvis.

'You're going to put her trunk in that box?' asked Mickey Thompson, doubtfully.

'But Purvis,' said Allen. 'It doesn't come off: it's *fixed*.'

'Of course not,' said Purvis. 'We'll use the box to make a dog outfit. Ortrud can wear it and her trunk will be hidden.'

'So will her eyes,' pointed out Allen.

'Yes, she'll **crash** about,' said Mickey Thompson. He made a **TRUMPETING** noise and **crashed** into Purvis, to demonstrate. There was a small s c u f f l e.

'I was about to say,' said Purvis, rolling off Mickey Thompson, 'that we can cut eyeholes. Then she'll be able to see.'

Everyone agreed it was worth a try, so they *tipped*

everything out

out of the box

and set to work. When they'd finished they put Ortrud into the cardboard dog outfit and stepped back to have a look at the effect.

'*Hmm*,' said Purvis.

'It's not *too* bad,' said Mickey Thompson.

'Um…' said Allen, 'I'm a little bit worried about the **tail**.'

Everyone looked at the back of the box and then back at Allen.

'It's just that it's supposed to be a **waggiest** *tail* competition,' explained Allen, 'but there isn't one.'

'Draw it on?' suggested Mickey Thompson.

'No, let's pull it through,' said Purvis.

So they made a small hole in the box and pulled Ortrud's tail through.

They all stood back to have another look.

'*Um,*' said Allen.

'What?' said the mice.

'I'm still a little bit worried about the *tail*,' said Allen, apologetically.

Everyone looked at Ortrud's tail and then at Allen.

'It's just…' said Allen.

'Just what?' said the mice.

'It's just that it's supposed to be *waggy*. Ortrud's tail is more kind of *swishy.*'

'He's right,' *sighed* Mickey Thompson.

'I think I'll make some more tea,' said Purvis.

So
he
made
a
fresh
pot
of tea

and everyone sat around thinking some more. 'There needs to be some kind of mechanism,' said Purvis, after a while. 'To make the tail waggier.'

'How about,' said Allen, 'instead of using Ortrud's tail, we make a pretend tail out of a brush or a stick or something, and someone sits inside the box and works it, waggily.'

'You might have something there, Allen,' said Mickey Thompson.

'I'll have another look under

Howard's desk,' said Purvis,
disappearing. After a lot of
rummaging, Purvis reappeared
brandishing an

old
toothbrush.

'Let's try this,' he said.

He climbed inside the box,
pulled Ortrud's tail in and pushed
the toothbrush out.

135

'What does it look like?' he **shouted.**

'A toothbrush,' **shouted** back Mickey Thompson.

'Try wagging it,' **shouted** Allen.

Purvis tried wagging it.

'Faster!' **shouted** Mickey Thompson.

Purvis wagged *faster*.

'Faster! Faster!' **shouted** Mickey Thompson, getting over-excited.

'I can't go any *faster,*' said Purvis.

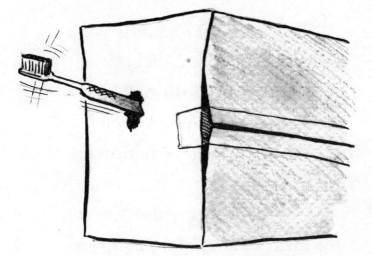

He stopped wagging and clambered out.

'So what do you think?' he puffed.

'I think your face has gone bright pink,' said Mickey Thompson, and there was another small scuffle.

'Well, I think it's a pretty good disguise,' said Allen, 'and that toothbrush tail works well.'

'Howard will be back soon,' said Purvis. 'Let's see if he notices it isn't Allen.'

So Allen hid _{under} the desk and the mice sat around trying to look as though everything was normal. The door opened and Howard came in.

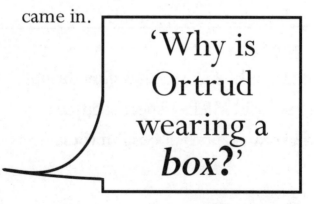

'Why is Ortrud wearing a *box*?'

said Howard.

'Oh, that isn't Ortrud,' said Mickey Thompson, airily. 'It's the dog, Allen.'

'Ah,' said Howard, 'Hello, Allen. And where might Ortrud be, do you suppose?'

There was an uncomfortable silence . . . . After what seemed like quite a long time, Purvis said:

'I think she might have just
stepped out for a walk.'

'Ah,' said Howard. 'I see.'

'Shall we put
the kettle on?'

offered Purvis, brightly.

'Please do,' said Howard, so the
mice went over to the kettle and
made some more tea.

140

'Bother,' *whispered* Mickey Thompson to Purvis. 'We should have made an Ortrud outfit for Allen.'

'There wasn't time,' *hissed* back Purvis.

'What's all the *whispering*?' said Howard.

'Nothing!' said the mice, **loudly**.

'Well now,' said Howard, settling down with his cup of tea. 'I hope Allen hasn't been too much trouble.'

'No trouble at all,' said Purvis.

'He's a dear.'

'Yes, isn't he?' said Howard.

Everyone watched as Howard sipped his tea. 'I had wondered…' said Howard, slowly.

'Yes?' said the mice, quickly.

'…Where that old toothbrush had got to.'

'What old toothbrush?' said Purvis, looking around.

'The one Allen seems to be, err, holding,' said Howard.

'That isn't a toothbrush, it's Allen's *tail*,' said Mickey Thompson.

142

'I don't think Allen will be very pleased to have his lovely tail mistaken for a toothbrush,' said Purvis, going up to Ortrud and patting the box. There was a muffled **TRUMPETING** noise from inside, and Mickey Thompson started to giggle.

'Right,' said Howard. 'Explanation, please. And do come out from under the desk, Allen, you'll get covered in dust.'

Allen came out, looking a bit sheepish.

'Allen doesn't want to take part in the competition,' **blurted** out Mickey Thompson.

'And he's been feeling **anxious** about it,' said Purvis.

'But he didn't want to disappoint you,' said Mickey Thompson.

'Oh dear,' said Howard. 'I had no idea. Err, how do you know all this?'

'He told us,' said Purvis. 'So we've—'

'Hang on,' said Howard. 'How do you mean, *"told"* you?

Did he speak to you?'

'That's right,' said Purvis, 'so we've—'

'With **words**, not **woofs**?' said Howard.

'Of course,' said Purvis. 'So anyway, we've made Ortrud a—'

'But Ortrud doesn't,' said Howard. *'Does she?'*

'Ortrud **TRUMPETS**,' said Mickey Thompson, **TRUMPETING**.

'Ortrud's too young to talk,' said Purvis. 'So, anyway, we've made her a dog outfit, so she can go instead.'

'*Eh?*' said Howard, rubbing at his head. 'Oh. Yes. Hmm.' He took a gulp of tea and then stood up and walked around Ortrud, examining the dog outfit from every angle.

'The thing is,' said Howard, eventually, 'it all needs to look far more woolly. Hang on.'

He rushed out of the room and everyone looked at each other.

'I think I'll make some more tea,'

said Mickey Thompson.

Suddenly there was the sound of

heavy footsteps

outside the door. Everyone froze.

'That isn't Howard,' said Purvis, as someone rattled the handle.

The mice and Allen dived under the desk . . .

. . . just as the door

burst open and

Mr Bullerton came in.

'Hah!' said Mr Bullerton,

triumphantly. *'Mess!'*

He went over to the box and

looked down at it, tutting.

Stay still, Ortrud, please stay

still, thought Purvis, holding his

breath.

Mr Bullerton

walked all

around the box,

still tutting, and then bent down
and picked something up from the
floor.

It was Allen's dog-show leaflet.
'*DOG WITH, the Waggiest...*
COMPETITION ...
Prizes ...'
read Mr Bullerton. '*Hmmm.*'

He folded it up and put it in his pocket. Then the door opened again and Howard came in

carrying an old brown blanket.

'Look what I found in the storeroom…' he began, '…oh dear, yes, ah, Mr Bullerton,' he   finished. **'Don't oh dear yes ah Mr Bullerton me,'** said Mr Bullerton. 'What's the meaning of it?'

'What's the m—' said Howard.
'THIS!' interrupted Mr
Bullerton, pointing at the box.
'This great pile of junk
in the middle of your
room. I've never seen
anything like it.'

'No,' said Howard. 'Neither have I.'

'Well, get rid of it,' said Mr
Bullerton, crossly. 'If I ever have to
set eyes on it again, you're for it.
And what are you doing with that
blanket?' he continued.

'Oh, err, I was a little chilly,'
said Howard.

'*A little chilly?*' said Mr Bullerton, going purple. 'A LITTLE *CHILLY*? It's practically the middle of summer.' Mr Bullerton put his face very close to Howard's.

'Just you listen to me,' he said. 'I don't pay you to loll around wrapped up in blankets. I pay you to work. Tidily. Without boxes. Without blankets. AND WITHOUT MESS. Get on with it.'
And Mr Bullerton *stomped* off, closing the door behind him

very loudly.

Allen and the mice came out from under the desk.

'Oh dear,' said Purvis.

'Never mind about that now,' said Howard. 'Let's try out this blanket.'

So they cut some eyeholes and a hole for the tail, and draped the blanket over Ortrud's box.

Everyone stepped back to look.

'Hmm,' said Howard. 'Ears.'

'Wait! I know!' said Purvis.

He dived under Howard's desk again and quickly reappeared

clutching an old pair of knitted mittens.

'I saw these under there earlier,' he said.

'Perfect,' said Howard, stapling them on to the costume. 'Now, what are we going to do about this **tail?**'

'The toothbrush wags well,'
said Mickey Thompson, to
Howard. 'Purvis sits inside and
works it.'

'The toothbrush is a good
foundation,' said Howard, 'but it
needs to be far more… err…
more… you know…' He waved
his hands about.

'Puffy?' said Mickey Thompson.

'Tufty?' said Purvis.

'No… err… more… err…'
said Howard.

'Fluffy?' said Mickey Thompson.

'Frondy?' said Purvis.

'*Woolly,*' said Howard, taking off his sock.

It was a brown woollen one. Howard stuck it on to the toothbrush and everyone stepped back again to have a look at the overall effect. 'Right,' said Howard. 'Now *that's* what I call a dog outfit.'

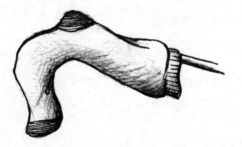

The Waggiest Tail

part 2

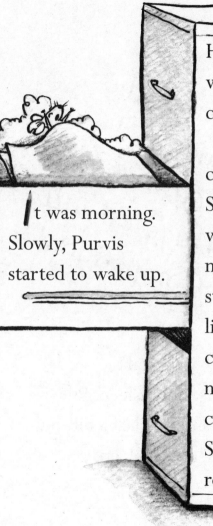

It was morning. Slowly, Purvis started to wake up.

He was feeling warm and comfortable, and wriggled contentedly. Slowly, Purvis woke up some more. He was starting to feel a little less comfortable, and not quite as contented. Suddenly he remembered:

it was the
day of the
Dog with the
Waggiest Tail
Competition!

Purvis sat up with a start.

Everyone else was asleep. Purvis shifted about and **coughed** a bit, but everyone else stayed asleep.

He climbed out of bed, rather **noisily**. He cl_att_ered around

finding mugs and making tea.

Nobody moved. Eventually, he went over to Mickey Thompson and prodded.

'Uff,' said Mickey Thompson.

'Mickey Thompson,' *whispered* Purvis.

'Umph,' said Mickey Thompson.

'Are you asleep?' said Purvis, quietly.

'Wuh?' said Mickey Thompson, drowsily.

'I SAID ARE YOU ASLEEP?' said Purvis, loudly.

Mickey Thompson sat up with a start, and Ortrud sat up with a trumpet.

'I was worried we'd be late,' explained Purvis, once Mickey Thompson and Ortrud had recovered.

TRUMPET.

'Oh well, now we're up we can have some **breakfast**,' said Mickey Thompson.

'I suppose we should,' said Purvis, 'but I don't feel hungry at all. My stomach's full of *butterflies*.'

'*Butterflies?*'
said Mickey
Thompson.

'Where did you get *butterflies* from?'

'They were there when I woke
up this morning,' said Purvis.

'But what did you go and *eat*
them for?' said Mickey Thompson.

'Eh?' said Purvis.

'And why the *whole lot*?
You could have saved some for
me.'

'You wouldn't have liked them,'
said Purvis. 'They're an Acquired
Taste. Especially the pretty yellow
ones,' he added, giggling.

Mickey Thompson bounced
Purvis and there was a small
scuffle.

'You don't want *butterflies*,'
said Purvis, once they'd finished.
'I'll make you and Ortrud some
porridge instead.'

165

So Ortrud and Mickey
Thompson tucked into

large bowls of
porridge

while Purvis drank a cup of tea.
  'I'll make up for it later, with
the picnic,' he said.

Afterwards, the mice dressed
Ortrud in the dog outfit and bus-
ied about preparing for the outing.
By the time Howard and Allen
arrived to collect them, they were
ready and waiting *excitedly* on
the desk. Purvis, looking **tense**,
was clutching a map and a small

notebook in which he'd written down a lot of research under the headings 'DOGS', and 'WAGGING', and 'COMPETITIONS'.

Mickey Thompson, looking *cheerful*, was wearing a flowery sun-hat and holding a picture he'd drawn of Allen.

'I'm going to wave it about, like a flag,' he told Howard.

'Good for you,' said Howard.

'Let's be off.'

So

they

all

trooped

out

of Howard's

office and up the **long**

corridor to the lift. The doors

pinged open and they

bundled in.

'Down, please!' said Purvis.

'Give me a chance,' said

Howard, 'I'm just about to

press—'

The lift started to trundle them downwards, **clunkily**.

'Thank you!' said Purvis.

'But I haven't pressed it yet!' said Howard.

'What a big hamper,' observed the lift.

'It's full of picnic,' confided Mickey Thompson. 'Purvis and Ortrud are taking part in a comp—'

'What?' said Howard.

'STOP!' said Purvis, *very loudly.*

The lift **jerked** to a halt and everyone fell over in a heap.

'What are you doing!?' squawked Howard.

'Quick! We need to go back up,' said Purvis. 'We've left Ortrud behind!'

So the lift took them back up. The doors *pinged* open and everyone b u n d l e d out and down the long corridor to Howard's office.

171

'You were talking to the *lift*!' said Howard, and they **hurried** along.

'Yes,' said Purvis. 'Don't you?'

'No!' said Howard.

'How does she know where to take you, then?' asked Purvis.

'The buttons!' said Howard. 'I *press* them.'

'Oh!' said Purvis. 'We wondered what those were for. It seems more friendly to ask though really, doesn't it?'

'I suppose so,' *sighed* Howard.

172

When they got back to the office Ortrud was asleep inside the dog outfit, snoring gently.

'*Phew,*' said Purvis. 'I was worried she'd think we'd forgotten her.'

'We *had* forgotten her,' pointed out Mickey Thompson.

'Never mind!' said Howard quickly, before a s^{c}u^{ff}l$_e$ could start. 'Let's get going or we'll be late.' Scooping Ortrud into his arms, he **dashed** off up the corridor to the lift. Everyone **dashed** after him.

'Oo, me **mechanism**,' groaned the lift, as she **clanked** them all downwards again.

'We'll save you a sandwich,' promised Purvis, 'to make up for all the extra upping and downing.'

When they reached the ground floor Howard *ushered* them outside to his car and they all climbed in and set off – Howard driving, Purvis calling out directions from his map, and everyone else looking out of the windows and enjoying the views.

'I'm still feeling nervous,' confessed Allen, 'even though I'm not the one having to take part.' Everyone reassured Allen that he wasn't the only one.

Before too long they arrived at a big field. Over the entrance fluttered a banner that said

FETE

and lower down was a smaller banner that said

DOG WITH THE WAGGIEST TAIL COMPETITION!!!

175

In the middle of the field was the competition show-ring and around the edges were a lot of stalls, and a lot of people milling about.

There were stalls selling toys, stalls selling

books,

and stalls selling homemade jam.

There was a **big** tent full of

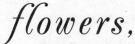

flowers,

and an even
bigger tent
full of cakes
and buns.

'Let's go in there first,' said
Mickey Thompson, pointing.

'Not so fast,' said Howard. 'If
you lot are set upon entering this
competition, we'll have to go and
register.'

So they joined a **long** queue of dogs and owners who were waiting to register.

'Oo, look!' said Mickey Thompson, as they neared the front. 'It's Mr Bullerton!'

'Oh no,' said Purvis.

'Oh dear,' said Allen.

'*Why me?*' groaned Howard.

Mr Bullerton was sitting behind a table with a stack of registration forms, looking pleased with himself. There was a **SMUG-LOOKING** dog sitting next to him.

'I didn't know he had a dog,' said Purvis.

'It looks like him!' said Mickey Thompson.

'Listen,' said Howard. 'There seems to be some kind of problem.'

Mr Bullerton was shaking his head at a woman who was trying to register. 'No no no,' he was saying.

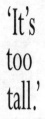

'It's
too
tall.'

'What do you mean?' said the woman.

'There's a height restriction,' said Mr Bullerton. 'It's in the rules.'

'My Susan has entered this competition every year since 1997,' said the woman. 'She's won it three times.'

'Not this year!' said Mr Bullerton. 'Next.'

'Well, really,' said the woman. She stalked off with a dejected-looking Susan, and a small boy approached the table carrying a **stout** and very waggy puppy.

'What's that?' said Mr Bullerton.

'My dog,' said the boy. 'He's called—"

'What breed?' **snapped** Mr Bullerton.

'Um, I think it's a spaniel,' said the boy.

'What kind of a spaniel?'

'Um, a Cocker Spaniel,' said the boy.

'That's the *wrong* kind of spaniel for this competition,' said

Mr Bullerton. 'Springer, or Water, not Cocker. Take it away.'

'But—'

'And he's too small. And **too fat.** Next!' said Mr Bullerton.

'Oh no,' gulped Allen. 'It's us.'

'Ah,' said Mr Bullerton, as they approached the table. 'It's Howard Armitage.'

'So it is!' said Howard.

'Planning on entering?' said Mr Bullerton.

'Well—'

'I shouldn't bother,' said Mr Bullerton. '*My* dog's going to win.'

He *glowered* at Allen, and Allen backed away slightly.

'No, this is the one,' said Howard, tapping the head-area of the box.

'*That?*' snorted Mr Bullerton. 'Doesn't stand a chance.'

He picked up his pen, and took a new form from the pile.

'Right. What kind of a dog is it?' he **demanded**, peering.

'It's a, err, a, err...' said Howard.

'A-err what?' said Mr Bullerton.

'*Boxer*,' whispered Purvis, who'd been frantically flipping through his research notes.

'Brilliant!' said Howard. 'Boxer!' He beamed at Mr Bullerton.

'I've never seen a Boxer-type-dog that looked like that before,' said Mr Bullerton, peering harder.

'Yes, well, it isn't *all* Boxer, clearly,' said Howard.

'It looks familiar but I can't quite—'

'YES,' shouted Howard. 'It's

half Boxer and half, err…'

'Half what?' said Mr Bullerton.

'Half, err, a, err…' said Howard.

Mr Bullerton **narrowed** his eyes at Howard.

'Elephant,' offered Mickey Thompson.

'EXPERIMENT,' said Howard, **loudly**. 'It was. One.'

'Hmm,' said Mr Bullerton. 'I'll put mongrel, shall I?'

'Please do,' said Howard.

Mr Bullerton wrote it down.

'And name,' said Mr Bullerton.

'Howard Armitage,' said Howard.

'Not you,' tutted Mr Bullerton.
'It.'

'Oh,' said Howard. 'Sorry.
Ortrud.'

'Or - *trud*,'
repeated Mr Bullerton,
writing.

'And Purvis,'

hissed

Mickey Thompson,
tugging at
Howard's
trousers.

'*Shoosh*,' said Howard.

'Don't you shoosh me,' said Mr Bullerton.

'Of course not,' said Howard. 'I was *shooshing* the dog.'

Mr Bullerton **glared** at him, and Mickey Thompson tugged again, **harder**.

'And Purvis,' sighed Howard.

'What? Which?'

'Both,' said Howard. 'The name's *Ortrud and Purvis*.'

'You're telling me that thing there's called Ortrudanpurvis,' said Mr Bullerton.

'The dog, yes,' confirmed Howard. He nodded at Mr Bullerton encouragingly, and patted the head-area of the box.

Breathing heavily, Mr Bullerton stared at Howard, then at Ortrud, then at Howard again. Still staring, he fumbled about on the tabletop, picked up a sticky label with the word

COMPETITOR

on it, and stared at that.

'Thank you,' said Howard, seizing the label and bustling everybody away.

'Do you think he suspected anything?' asked Purvis, as they hurried off.

'Hazard a wild guess,' replied Howard, a little tensely. 'I need tea.'

So they had a cup of tea

and some picnic, and then it was time for the competition to begin. Howard stuck the sticky label on to Ortrud, and Purvis climbed inside the box and gripped the toothbrush.

Everyone **clapped** and **cheered** as Howard led Ortrud into the ring with the other competitors. There was more **clapping** and **cheering** as the judge arrived, who was a **Very Important Person** and whose job it was to choose the **waggiest** tail, Allen explained to Mickey Thompson.

'Right,' said the judge. 'Dogs: get ready to **wag**, and when I blows… *Go!*' and he gave a very **LOUD** blast on a whistle.

Ortrud leapt
into the air
with a **startled**

TRUMPET

and **shot off** across the field,

dragging Howard with her.

All the dogs **charged** after
them, barking joyfully.

'Oh dear,' said Allen.

Everyone watched open-
mouthed as Ortrud and Howard

crashed through
the jam stall, disappeared into the

flower tent and re-emerged
covered in marigolds.

'Her costume's slipped,' said
Mickey Thompson. 'She can't see
out.'
TRUMPETING wildly,
Ortrud *galloped* back into the
show-ring, ran around in a small

circle three times and hurtled off
sideways into the buns tent,
pursued by Howard and the dogs.

'Oh no!' gasped Allen.

There was a lot of **woofing**
and **TOOTING** and *crashing*
and then Howard burst
out of the tent and sprinted
across the field.

'Howard's got cream
bun all over his head!'
shouted Mickey Thompson, who
was *enjoying* himself hugely.

Swerving sharply, Howard narrowly
missed the judge, tripped over a

sausage dog that had suddenly changed direction, and **collided** with Mr Bullerton. With a *roar* of fury Mr Bullerton **lunged** at Howard and the two of them staggered, and fell and disappeared from view as the dogs piled on and set to work licking.

Meanwhile, Ortrud had ambled out of the buns tent carrying a large slice of Dundee cake.

'Ortrud,' called Mickey Thompson. 'Over here.'

She trotted over, and Purvis plopped out of the box and lay on the grass, panting hotly.

'Purvis!' said Mickey Thompson. 'Are you all right?'

'Yes,' puffed Purvis, 'but what's up with *him*?' he asked, pointing at Allen, who was rolling about on the ground, thumping his tail and making a *whooping* noise.

'He's laughing,' said Mickey Thompson. 'Look at his tail go!'

Just then there was another odd noise as Howard crawled over, **groaning.**

'I'm so pleased you're all enjoying yourselves,' said Howard, and everyone **laughed** even harder.

'*Look,*' said Purvis, sitting up and wiping his eyes. 'What's happening now?'

Mr Bullerton had managed to get out from underneath the dogs and was in the middle of the show-ring waving his arms about.

'Ladies and gentlemen,' he announced. 'Due to **unforeseen circumstances**, we're **unable** to decide on a **winner** this year.'

'Wait!' said the judge, and pointed at Allen.

'No!' said Mr Bullerton.

'Yes!' said the judge.

'Him.'

'But he isn't even registered!' **_roared_** Mr Bullerton. 'It's against the rules.'

'Oh, don't talk nonsense,' said the judge, handing Allen an **enormous** tin of biscuits.

'He's definitely got the **waggiest** tail of all.'

And he had!

'Marvellous,' said Howard, hurriedly gathering together mice and Allens and biscuits and Ortruds and pieces of cake.

'Now let's get out of here, *fast*.'

And they did.